ERIC and the VOICE OF DOOM

Collect them all!

Eric and the Striped Horror
Eric and the Wishing Stone
Eric and the Pimple Potion
Eric and the Green-Eyed God
Eric and the Voice of Doom

No. 1 Boy Detective series:

The Disappearing Daughter
The Popstar's Wedding
How To Be a Detective
Spycatcher
Serious Graffiti
Dog Snatchers
Under Cover
Gruesome Ghosts
Football Forgery
The Mega Quiz

For older readers:

Billy's Blitz
Dangerous Diamonds
Run Rabbit Run
Secret Suffragette
Storm Runners
A Twist of Fortune

ERIC and the VOICE OF DOOM

BARBARA MITCHELHILL
Illustrated by Tony Ross

Andersen Press
LONDON

For the girls of Seaton House School – especially Karis, who thought of the blanket

This edition published in Great Britain in 2020 by
Andersen Press Limited
20 Vauxhall Bridge Road
London SW1V 2SA
www.andersenpress.co.uk

First published in 2001 by Andersen Press Limited

2 4 6 8 10 9 7 5 3 1

British Library Cataloguing in Publication Data available.

ISBN 978 1 78344 956 9

Printed and bound in Great Britain
by Clays Limited, Elcograf S.p.A.

ONE

The hall at North Street School was buzzing with excitement. Who had won the Battle of the Bands competition? That's what all the kids wanted to know. Six bands had entered. One of them was Eric's The Ez Effect. And he was in the crowd, staring up at the empty stage.

'How do you think we did?' he whispered in Wesley's ear.

Wesley shrugged. 'OK, I suppose.'

'Only OK?' said Eric, whizzing round to face him. 'Only OK?'

Wesley grinned. 'You were brilliant, Ez. You're really cool on the guitar.'

'So you think we might win, eh Wez?'

'Yeah. We were loads better than the other bands,' said Wez. 'Brent Dwyer's was rubbish.'

Eric was about to say something meaningful and modest when he felt a hand grab hold of his neck.

'Did you say my band's rubbish?' growled Brent Dwyer, who was standing behind them. Eric's blood ran cold. Brent squeezed tighter and the air in Eric's windpipe was almost cut off. He grabbed Wez too so that they dangled in Brent's grasp like a pair of turnips.

'You won't win,' he said, bashing them together. 'No way!'

Eric was on the verge of passing out for lack of oxygen, when Mrs Cracker (known as the Big Cheese) marched onto the stage. Brent let go and Eric and Wez dropped to the floor as Craig Newman (lead singer of The Power) followed the Head. At the sight of him some of the girls started to scream and pretended to faint.

'Pathetic!' wheezed Eric, looking up from the floor as the noise continued.

The Big Cheese flapped her hands for everyone to calm down. 'This has been an exciting afternoon,' she said, beaming down at the crowd of faces. 'Craig has listened to the bands and now he will tell you who has won today and will go through to the final.'

Eric and Wez struggled to their feet. They grinned and nudged each other as the pop star walked to the front of the stage.

Then there was more girlie screaming.

'I wish they'd shut up,' said Eric. Wez agreed.

Eventually, after a lot of shushing, the hall went quiet.

'I'll talk about the bands one by one,' Craig said. And he did. Slowly and carefully. Describing good points and bad points.

'This is dead boring,' Eric whispered. 'Why doesn't he just say who came first?'

At last, Craig pulled a gold envelope from his pocket containing the name of the winner. They all held their breath as he passed it to Mrs Cracker.

'Oh my goodness!' the Head giggled. 'This is just like the Oscars!'

She tore the envelope open and took out a piece of paper. 'The winner is . . .' She paused dramatically. 'Eric Braithwaite and his band – The Ez Effect.'

The cheers were nearly as loud as they had been for Craig Newman. But Eric noticed that nobody screamed or fainted.

'Nice one, Ez!' everyone shouted, slapping him on the back as he pushed through the crowd. Then, Wez (who played second guitar) and Kylie Partridge (drums) and Kelvin Thomas (keyboard) followed him onto the stage.

'Well done, guys!' said Craig as he shook their hands and gave Eric the silver Area Winner's Plate.

This was what he wanted. A chance to be a pop star. If everything went well from now on, he'd soon be on the telly!

TWO

After school, Eric had tea at Wez's house. His mum did the best chips – brown and crisp outside and white and soggy inside. Just the way he liked them.

'How's your mum today?' Mrs Robertson asked as she passed the tomato ketchup. 'I expect she's feeling really tired.'

Eric looked up. 'OK, thanks,' he said and loaded his fork with a small mountain of chips.

Why was it, he wondered, that everybody asked about Mum? Nobody asked how *he* felt. If they had, he would have said:

1. It was embarrassing that Mum was having a baby at her age.
2. That the thought of having a brother was a nightmare.

But nobody cared about him and he was very depressed.

Mrs Robertson smiled. 'You must be excited, Eric. It's lovely having a baby in the family!'

Wez suddenly sat up and looked alarmed. 'We're not having any more are we, Mum?'

Before she could answer, her phone rang. She picked it up and started chatting.

Meanwhile, the boys had a competition to see who could stuff the most chips in their mouth.

Then Mrs Robertson handed Eric the phone. 'It's your stepdad,' she said. 'He wants to speak to you.'

'Ask him if you can stay late, Ez,' said Wesley through a mouthful of chips.

'You're more than welcome to stay as long as you like, Eric,' said Mrs Robertson.

Not wanting to waste the chips, Eric quickly swallowed them before putting the phone to his ear. He listened for a while, and when he handed the phone back he was grinning.

'He's taking Mum to hospital. And guess what? He says I can stay the night at your house! Brilliant, eh? Can I sleep in the top bunk?'

'I'll toss you for it!' said Wez.

That night when they went to bed, they ate chocolate toffees, discussed being famous and twanged their guitars . . . until Wez's sister, Holly, came in, carrying a large stuffed lion.

'I want to come to your party,' she said.

Wesley was furious.

'It's not a party! Anyway, you're too young.'

'I'm five!'

'Go back to bed. We're talking boys' stuff.'

Holly stuck out her bottom lip. 'I'll tell Mum you're making a lot of noise.'

'Don't be stupid.'

'Give me a chocolate or I will!'

Wesley shook his head. 'No way!'

'I'll scream!' she said and turned to the door.

'All right!' Wez said and threw a sweet across the room. 'But it's my last one. Now go away.'

She had no intention of going away. She stood there, slowly unwrapping the gold paper.

Then Wesley's baby sister, Sammy, arrived.

'What oo doin', Hol?' she said.

'We're having a party – but you can't come. You're too young. And you can't have a sweet either. I got the last one.' And she popped it in her mouth.

Sammy's eyes grew wide with disappointment, her face crumpled and a loud wail erupted from her mouth.

Wez and Eric dived under their duvets as they heard Mrs Robertson thundering upstairs. She burst into the room, picked up the smallest child, grabbed the next size up and marched them back to bed.

Ten minutes later, Mrs Robertson returned.

'Wesley! Eric!' she whispered angrily.

They pretended to be asleep. But Wez's mum knew better. 'Upsetting the girls like that. How could you?!'

She went on and on until she ran out of steam. Then she walked out and switched off the light.

'Phew!' said Eric in the dark. 'Your sisters get you into loads of trouble, Wez.'

'Don't I know it?!'

Eric sighed. 'Girls are a pain, aren't they?'

'The worst.'

'I'm glad Mum's having a boy.'

'How do you know?'

'Well, she said she didn't ask the doctor because she wanted it to be a surprise, but then her friend did a test. She held a piece of string with a needle on the end over Mum's stomach and it went round and round.'

'What? The baby?'

'No. The needle. It's a sure sign it'll be a boy. Mum told me.'

'Well, that's all right then,' said Wez. 'Lucky you!'

And they fell asleep.

THREE

The next day was Saturday. Mrs Robertson opened the bedroom door and called in.

'Are you awake, Eric?' She sounded friendly. She must have forgotten about last night.

'Mmmmm,' Eric moaned as politely as he could. Being woken at nine o'clock on a Saturday was not fun.

She pulled back the curtains and painful rays of light struck Eric's eyelids.

'Wake up!' she said. 'You've got a busy day. Your stepdad's coming round at ten.'

Blinking at the light, Eric levered himself up onto his elbow. 'Can't I stay a bit longer, Mrs Robertson? Me and Wez were going to practise our guitars.'

'No, you can't!' she laughed. 'You've got more important things to do. You'll see.'

Then she left the room and went downstairs.

Wez, who had been woken by his mother's chatter, struggled to sit up. 'It's a bit inconsiderate, Ez. Why's he coming round this early?'

'Dunno. You can never tell why grown-ups do anything.'

When they went down to the kitchen, Mrs Robertson was singing loudly and setting cereal bowls on the table.

Before Eric and Wez were half way through breakfast, The Bodge arrived. (Eric always thought of him as The Bodge, even though he wasn't his teacher any more. Even though he was married to his mum.)

Eric looked up from his plate. What a shock! The Bodge looked awful! He had terrible bags under his eyes and his face looked chalk white. It was enough to put Eric off his food. It was obvious he should have stayed in bed.

'Hello, Eric,' he said. 'Did you have a good time last night?'

'Great!' Eric said, anxious to finish his toast and marmalade breakfast. 'But I don't have to go home, do I?'

The Bodge glanced at Wesley's mum and smiled.

'I thought you'd want to come to the hospital to see the new addition.'

Eric looked puzzled but continued eating, not wanting to waste a good breakfast.

'Your mum had the baby last night!' he said, ruffling Eric's hair. 'Don't you want to see them?'

Eric wasn't keen but The Bodge was obviously expecting him to be excited.

'OK,' he said, when he'd wiped the last crumb of toast from his mouth. 'I'll go.' It was the least he could do, he thought.

At the hospital, Mum was in bed, her eyes closed. Some people have all the luck, thought Eric – having a good lie-in on a Saturday morning!

The Bodge raised a finger to his lips. 'Ssh! Mum's resting. Let's look at the baby.'

Next to Mum's bed, in a plastic box on wheels, Eric saw a tiny, shrivelled, red-faced thing with puffy eyes. It was quite a shock. Did newborn babies really look as bad as this? He had never seen anything like it – except when the school mouse had her litter last summer.

Mum woke up and smiled. 'What do you think of the baby, Eric?'

'Yeah,' he said. 'OK.' He couldn't think of anything else to say.

Mum held her arms out to give him a hug. 'So you like her then?'

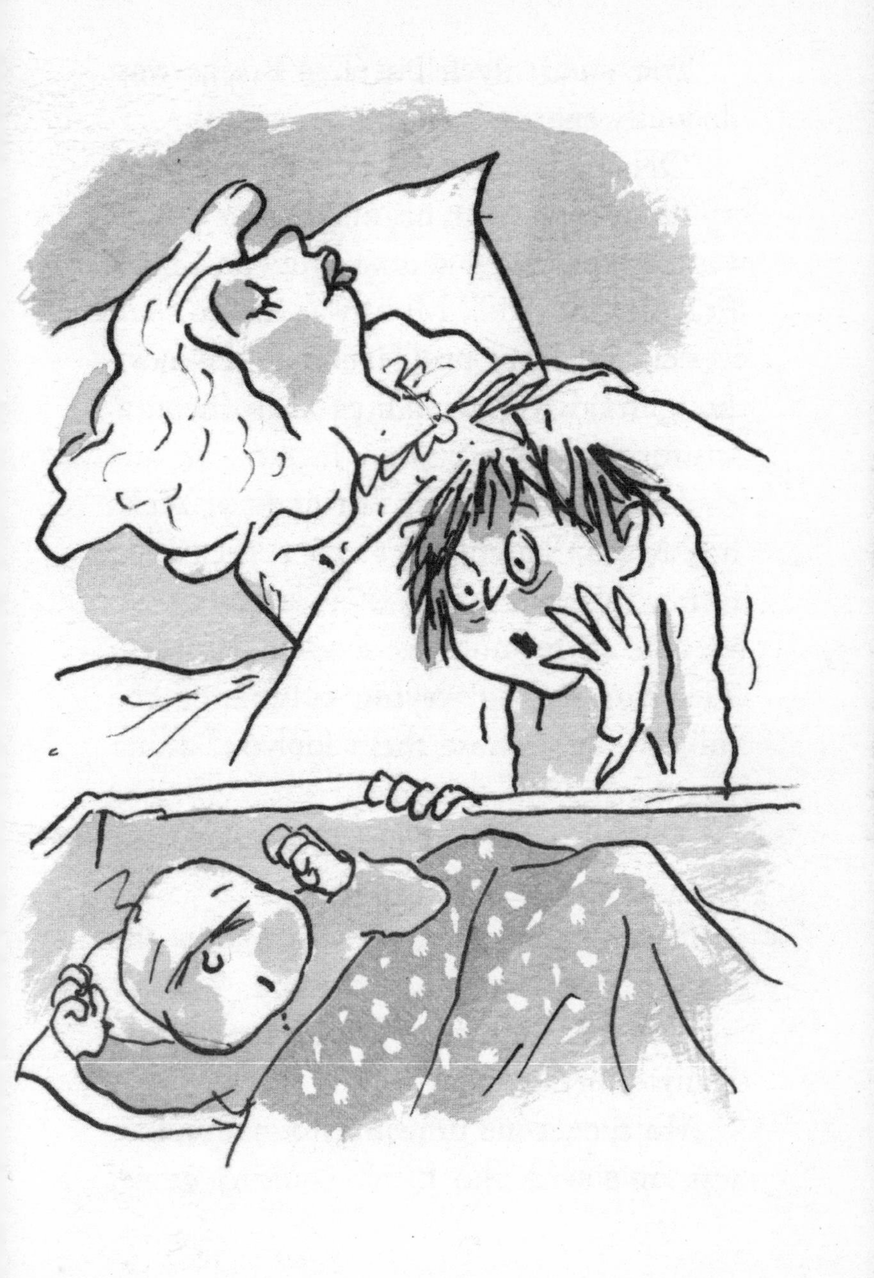

Eric suddenly felt a terrible sensation down his spine.

'What d'you mean "HER"?'

'Your little sister, of course,' said Mum.

'But you said it was going to be a boy!' Eric protested.

She shook her head. 'How could I know, duck? You know we wanted a surprise.'

Eric was very upset. In fact, he was choked. Remembering last night at Wez's house, the thought of having a sister filled him with horror.

'We've brought you some flowers,' The Bodge said, trying to change the subject. 'Eric chose them for you, didn't you, son?'

As well as the bouquet, he handed her a parcel wrapped in brown paper.

Mum looked at the writing on the front. 'That's from Rose,' she said. 'I expect it's a present for the baby. All the way from South America.'

For the second time in ten minutes, Eric was rigid with shock. He couldn't move.

He couldn't speak. A present from Auntie Rose. That's all he needed! Everything that she had sent so far had turned Eric's world upside-down. Not just that jumper he had called the Striped Horror. No, there had been more. The Wishing Stone and the Pimple Potion. And as for that fertility symbol she had sent as Mum's wedding present . . . well, here was the baby to prove its power.

Eric felt sick. The present would have serious consequences. He just knew it!

FOUR

When the baby came home from hospital, Eric had a terrible time. Night after night, she woke him with her crying. He felt exhausted and sometimes fell asleep in lessons. His new teacher Miss Borrage was fantastic. She knew what he was going through and let him off some of his homework. Why couldn't Mum be like that? She was so snappy these days. She wouldn't even let him practise the guitar.

'Just stop it, Eric!' she said a hundred times a day. 'You'll wake the baby.'

It was hopeless! The house wasn't the same. It was full of baby smells and baby noises and nappies and clothes. There was no room for his stuff any more.

The Bodge tried to help.

'How about playing your guitar in the shed, Eric? It'll be quiet there.'

But the weather was cold and he couldn't play with freezing fingers.

'I'm fed up,' he said to Wez one day. 'There's only one week to the Battle of the Bands National Final. We don't stand a chance if we don't practise.'

'Miss Borrage might help,' said Wez.

Eric nodded. She was his guardian angel. She smiled at him so often, he just knew she understood how he was suffering. Of course she would help.

'I'm the leader. I'll go and ask her if there's somewhere we could practise.'

After school, he carried Miss Borrage's bag to the car. (He didn't care that it was extremely heavy.)

Then he asked her.

'Just for you, Eric!' she said, smiling down at him. 'You can use the music room on Saturday morning.'

'Thanks!' said Eric. Miss Borrage was the best teacher ever!

When he got home, Mum was busy trying to get the baby to sleep.

'Do me a favour, Eric,' she said wearily. 'Push her round the back garden for me. Maybe she'll drop off.'

Eric was in such a good mood that he agreed. Mum tucked the baby in the pram and covered her with a blanket.

'I'll make myself a cup of tea,' she said. 'I haven't had one all day.'

'Can I have some crisps?' he said and Mum passed a packet over to him.

Once outside on the path, he jiggled the pram handle with one hand and dipped into the crisps with the other. The baby's eyes were closing already. Looking after babies was dead easy, he thought.

But the baby didn't fall asleep. Suddenly, her eyes shot open and stared at him.

Maybe she was bored. He leaned forward and jiggled a string of yellow plastic ducks. She stared at them and then she smiled! Eric was very pleased with himself.

'Ducks,' he said clearly. 'Yellow ducks.'

The baby looked up at him.

'Ducks,' Eric repeated. 'Do you like the ducks, eh?'

The baby smiled again.

'Ooh yeth, Ewic,' she said. 'I like duckth.'

The bag of crisps fell from his grasp. His mouth dropped open. Had he heard right?

'W-what did you say?'

The baby gurgled. 'I thed I like duckth. Ethpethly yellow oneth.'

It was too much for him. He abandoned the pram and ran indoors.

'MUM!' he yelled as he raced through the kitchen. 'MUM! YOU'RE NOT GOING TO BELIEVE THIS.'

Mum was sitting with her feet up on the settee, looking very tired.

'Calm down, Eric. What is it?'

'The baby's talking, that's what! She said she liked ducks!'

Mum sighed deeply. It was clear from the look on her face that she didn't believe a word. She swung her feet off the settee and stood up.

'Can't I even have a cup of tea in peace?' she said. 'If you didn't want to look after the baby, you should have said so.'

Eric felt depressed and retreated to his room where he sat on the bed. Had he really heard the baby speak? Or was it just that the sleepless nights were getting to him?

FIVE

The Bodge looked at Eric with a concerned expression. He must have noticed that Eric was feeling tired and miserable.

'There's a fair in town tomorrow, Eric,' he said. 'We could all go after school.'

Mum smiled. 'You'd like that, wouldn't you, love?'

'Will we have to take the baby?' Eric asked.

Mum nodded.

'Couldn't she stay at home?'

'She can't be left alone,' said The Bodge.

Eric tried arguing, but it was no use. The baby had to come.

The next day, when tea was finished, they got ready to go.

'Put your coat on, son,' said The Bodge.

'There's a cold wind blowing.'

Eric fetched his padded jacket, Mum put on her new red coat and wrapped the baby up warm in the pram.

'Look at her clutching the blanket with her little fingers,' said Mum, as they walked down the street. 'It was a lovely present – don't you think so, Eric?'

'What?'

'The blanket,' she said. 'Auntie Rose sent it.'

At the mention of Auntie Rose, Eric's brain began to spin. He might have guessed! The blanket had some kind of spookiness in it. It had made a four-week-old baby talk.

As they walked into the fairground, Mum didn't notice Eric was distracted.

'What ride are you going on first, love?' Mum asked him.

'Dunno,' he said. 'I'll wait a bit.'

'Well, I'd like to go on the dodgems,' she laughed. 'Are you coming on with me, Brian? Eric can have the pram for a few minutes.'

'But I . . .'

'Get yourself an ice cream, son.' The Bodge said. 'That'll cheer you up.' And he handed him some money.

Before Eric knew it, Mum and The Bodge were whirling round in a small red car, laughing as they bumped into the others. Miserably, Eric pushed the pram a little way to the ice cream van and bought a Mr Whippy. It made him feel better for a moment.

But not for long. The baby spoke again.

'I want a duck, Ewic,' she said.

Eric almost dropped his ice cream. He looked down at her in amazement. She was pointing towards the hook-a-duck stand where yellow plastic ducks were floating on water.

'You can't have one,' he said. 'I'm not allowed to go too far.'

'Pleeth, Ewic. I like duckth.'

'No! I said no and I mean no!'

She stuck out her bottom lip and he knew she was going to howl very loudly.

'Have some ice cream,' he said and pushed it into her hand.

She smiled and began to lick it.

'Like it!' she said.

Eric felt relieved. But in no time at all, the baby's face was smeared in sticky ice cream.

Before he could clean her up, Mum's ride had finished and she was back.

'Eric! What have you been doing?' she said, pushing him aside. 'Babies shouldn't have ice cream. It makes them ill.'

She bent over to wipe her face.

Eric crossed his fingers, hoping the baby would speak. At least Mum would find out he'd been telling the truth, after all.

'I don't know, Eric!' said Mum. 'I can't trust you to look after your sister for two seconds.'

As Mum gave her a final wipe, the baby began to make terrible faces as if she was in pain. Suddenly, she opened her mouth and the contents of her stomach erupted all over Mum's new coat.

'Oh dear!' said The Bodge. 'She's been sick.'

'I CAN SEE SHE'S BEEN SICK!' Mum shrieked. 'It's all Eric's fault! We're going home! I've had enough!'

They turned to go and Eric wondered if life could be more miserable than this.

SIX

That night, Eric lay in his bed, thinking about the band. They were meeting at school at ten o'clock to rehearse for two hours. Miss Borrage would be there and she would be really impressed.

'Here's to The Ez Effect!' he said to himself. 'Winners of the Battle of the Bands! Yeah!' He smiled and rolled over to get some sleep. He wanted to be on top form.

Although he tried, sleep wouldn't come. He counted a hundred sheep. He read five comics. He ate two bags of crisps. But nothing worked. He couldn't stop thinking about the baby. It seemed that she was programmed to get him into trouble. Like some annoying little robot.

Eventually he gave up on sleep.

'The only thing to do,' he said to himself, 'is to get that blanket.'

He slipped out of bed, slowly opened the door and peeped out. The house was quiet. The landing was dark. Eric tiptoed towards the spare bedroom and pushed the door open.

By the light of a small pink lamp, he could see the baby fast asleep in her cot, covered with Auntie Rose's blanket. Brilliant!

Eric leaned over and began to tug.

Slowly the cover began to move but, just when he thought he had it, the baby's eyes opened.

'Ewic!' she said. 'Have you come to pway?'

'No I haven't come to play,' he hissed. 'I came to . . . er . . . change your blanket.'

'Why?'

'Er . . . It needs washing.'

'But I'll be vewy cold without it.'

'Well, I'll give you another one.'

She stared at him and a tear trembled on her lashes. 'But I like this one, Ewic. It's vewy nithe.'

'Well, I'm going to have it,' he said and tugged hard.

The baby stared at him. 'I'll cwy!' she said and opened her mouth wide.

He knew Mum would be here like a shot if she heard. It was the worst thing that could happen.

'No!' said Eric. 'OK! OK! I won't take it.'

She closed her mouth and smiled up at him.

'All wight,' she said. 'I won't cwy.'

Eric breathed a sigh of relief and was about to go back to his room when the baby spoke again.

'Ewic,' she said. 'Will you take me to see the duckth?'

'What ducks?'

'The oneth in the park.'

'When?'

'Tomowow.'

'Tomorrow? No way! I can't.'

Immediately, she screwed up her eyes and opened her mouth wide again.

'OK. OK. You win,' he said. 'But we'll have to go early. I've got a rehearsal at ten.'

'Goody!' she squealed. 'You're such a luverly bwother, Ewic!'

And with that, she curled up in her cot, clutching the blanket.

SEVEN

It was a great sacrifice! Getting up early on Saturday morning.

By eight o'clock, Eric was dressed and ready to take the baby to the park. Out and back by ten. That was the plan.

Down in the kitchen, the baby was sleeping in her pram, tucked up in Auntie Rose's blanket. As Eric walked in, she opened her eyes.

'Can we go to see the duckth now, Ewic?' she said, smiling at him.

'When I've had my breakfast,' he said.

'Now! Now! Now!'

Just then, Mum walked in through the back door, carrying a clothes basket. She smiled at Eric and cooed at the baby.

'You wouldn't believe a baby could make so much washing,' she said as she passed through to the hall. Eric glanced at his sister. But she didn't speak.

'Make me a cup of tea, will you, love?' Mum called. 'I'm tired out.'

Eric sighed. She wasn't the only one! He had hardly slept! Who would have thought that a tiny, helpless baby could force him – a grown boy – to do things he didn't want to?

Then it struck him that he was being ridiculous. Of course she couldn't force him! What could she do if he walked out? Nothing! That's what!

He went and filled the kettle and switched it on. But when he turned back, the pram was empty. He panicked. Where was she? How could a four-week-old baby get out?

'I'm here, Ewic,' she said as if she could read his mind.

She was sitting on the floor on the far side of the kitchen. Worse still – she was holding Mum's best crystal vase.

‘Take me to the duckth, Ewic,’ she said, ‘or I’ll dwop it.’

Eric was gobsmacked! If she smashed the vase – who would get the blame? HE WOULD! This was pure blackmail!

‘All right! All right!’ he said. ‘I’ll take you if you put it down.’

‘NOW!’ she yelled, holding the vase over her head.

‘OK. OK!’ said Eric. ‘We’ll go now. But I’ll have to tell Mum.’

Mum walked back in just as the kettle boiled. ‘What will you have to tell Mum?’ she asked.

Eric busied himself making the tea, hoping Mum wouldn’t see his sister on the floor.

‘Er . . . I was thinking of taking the baby for a walk,’ he said as he put the mug on the table. ‘Give you a bit of a rest.’

‘That is thoughtful of you, love,’ said Mum and she flopped onto a chair.

Once her back was turned, Eric grabbed the baby and dumped her into the pram.

‘Right!’ he said. ‘I’ll take her now.’

Mum looked up from her tea. ‘Not yet, Eric. I’ve got to feed her. It won’t take long. Just let me finish my cuppa.’

Eric paced the floor while Mum drank her tea . . . gave the baby some milk . . . and changed her nappy. He could have done it twenty times faster! When she had finished, it was quarter past nine. Doom! He’d have to run all the way to the park.

When he was out on the street, he suddenly felt it wasn't cool to be seen pushing a baby. This was not how a future pop star should behave. He pulled his baseball cap over his forehead. Heavy disguise! Maybe no one would recognise him.

No such luck!

'Hey, Eric!' called a familiar voice. 'Whatcha doing with that pram? Are you playing Mummies and Daddies?'

It was Brent Dwyer! Of all the people in the world, it had to be him. Now everyone would know that ace guitarist Ez Braithwaite was a babysitter. Soon he'd be a laughing stock.

EIGHT

Eric raced towards the park, trying to make up for lost time.

'WHEEEEEEEE!' cried the baby as the pram whizzed along. 'Keep going, Ewic! I like it!'

By the time they got there, Eric was out of breath.

'This is it . . .' (gasp!) 'You can look . . .' (gasp!) 'at the ducks for . . .' (gasp!) 'five minutes . . .' (gasp!) 'and then we go home!' (double gasp!)

He left the pram on the path where she could see the pond. Then he flopped on a bench to recover his breath and closed his eyes for a second.

When he opened them again he was horrified! The pram was heading towards

the pond . . . The baby was sitting up . . . She was clinging onto the sides . . .

Eric leaped to his feet. 'Stop!' he yelled and raced after her. He had to get her before she reached the water.

But the baby was having a great time. 'Hey duckie-duckieth!' she called as the pram zipped along the path. 'I's coming to pway wiv you.'

Then *SPLASH!* The pram hit the water. The ducks quacked in a deafening chorus, flapped their wings and paddled off. The pram floated after them.

Luckily the park keeper was on the other side and saw what had happened. He dived into the pond – fully clothed.

'All right, my little lovely,' he called as he swam through the weed-infested water. 'I'll get you back to your mummy soon.'

Eric raced round the pond and was waiting when the park keeper emerged, dripping with slimy mud and dragging the pram after him. When he saw Eric standing there, he did not look pleased.

'Are you in charge of this baby?' he snapped.

Eric nodded nervously.

'THEN YOU OUGHT TO BE ASHAMED OF YOURSELF!' he shouted. 'Where do you live?'

When Eric said, 'Thirty-four Corporation Street,' the angry park keeper marched him back home. Then . . .

1. The park keeper knocked on the door.
2. Mum opened the door.
3. Mum listened to the park keeper.
4. Mum went mad at Eric.
5. The park keeper went mad at Eric.
6. Eric was sent to his room.

He would never make it to the rehearsal now!

He wasn't allowed out until twelve o'clock. Then he raced down to the school to explain what had happened.

Wez and the rest of the band were sitting by the gate. Brent Dwyer was with them and some other kids he wished would disappear.

‘Well, look who it is!’ Brent Dwyer shouted. ‘Only two hours late!’

‘I had to . . .’

‘Don’t tell us any lies, Eric Braithwaite,’ said Kelvin, standing up to face him. ‘Brent saw you in the park.’

‘But . . .’

‘We heard! You were playing by the pond!’ Kylie interrupted. ‘Miss Borrage is really mad with you, too! You don’t care about the band.’

'I helped out at the rehearsal,' sneered Brent Dwyer. 'Lucky I brought my guitar.'

Normally, they wouldn't let Brent near the band – but they were so angry with Eric that they had let him play.

Eric tried to speak.

'We don't want to talk to you,' said Kelvin. 'We just don't want you in the band.'

With that he and Kylie walked away and the rest followed.

Only Wez stayed behind.

'We're all a bit fed up, Ez,' he said. 'What really happened?'

Eric hung his head. 'It's a long story, Wez,' he said. 'It's another of Auntie Rose's presents.'

Wez nodded knowingly. 'Then it's Trouble with a capital T, Ez. Tell me about it.'

They sat down on the wall and Eric explained how his four-week-old sister could talk and sit up and even somehow get out of her pram.

'That's weird, Ez!'

'I know,' Eric continued. 'The problem is – she's blackmailing me, now. She gets me into trouble if I don't do what she wants. So what can I do, Wez?'

Wesley thought for a minute.

'Easy!' he said. 'You just wash the blanket.'

'Why?'

'Remember the Striped Horror lost its power when it was washed? Well . . .'

Eric's shoulders drooped. 'No good, Wez. I can't get it. I've already tried.'

'That's bad, Ez,' said Wesley, shaking his head from side to side. 'You're already in trouble with the band and Miss Borrage. It looks as if things can only get worse.'

NINE

It was the end for Eric. The band had finished with him. He was in deep trouble with everybody. And – the worst thing – he faced years of being blackmailed by his baby sister. There was only one thing to do . . .

He would leave home!

The sooner he left, the sooner Mum would find out the truth about the baby. She would feel really bad and spend weeks searching for him. Then, when she had found him, she would fling herself at this feet – sobbing – and beg him to come home.

Suddenly, Eric felt better.

That night, he packed his sports bag, ready to go. He filled it with two bumper bags of crisps from his emergency store, his top ten favourite comics and his

best football strip. At the last minute he squeezed in a spare pair of socks.

As he opened the bedroom door, he picked up his guitar. 'This should be good for busking,' he said to himself. 'I could earn a fortune!'

He stepped out onto the landing and tiptoed towards the top of the stairs. Everywhere was silent. Everyone was fast asleep . . . except the baby!

'Ewic!' she called. 'Ewic, come and pway wiv me.'

He rushed into her room. 'All right!' he whispered. 'But don't make a sound.'

She smiled. 'Pway me a tune, Ewic!' she said, pointing to his guitar. 'Thing to me!'

'I can't,' he hissed. 'Mum and The Bodge will wake up.'

The baby opened her mouth wide as if she was about to yell.

'No!' Eric pleaded. 'Don't cry.'

'I will if you don't pway your guitar, Ewic!'

In desperation, he gave in.

'If you promise to be good, I'll take you downstairs and play to you.'

The baby smiled and held up her arms to be picked up.

Eric carried her downstairs wrapped in the blanket and put her on the settee. Then he went back and fetched his bag and guitar.

'What'th in that bag?' the baby asked.

'Nothing.'

Eric opened it and she saw the crisps.

'I like cwisps,' she said.

'You're too young,' Eric protested.

'Want some,' she said and Eric gave in, again. It was the only way to stop her from yelling.

'Thing to me, Ewic,' she said as she took the first crisp out of the packet.

Eric decided that if he played something quiet, nobody upstairs would hear. So he sang, 'Twinkle, Twinkle Little Star'.

'Again!' the baby said when he had finished.

He had sung it eleven times and was very bored indeed, when he suddenly realised she had fallen asleep. Not only that, but she had a crisp in one hand and the packet in the other. For the first time in weeks, she was not holding onto the blanket! Now was his chance. Carefully, he tugged at it and, bit by bit, it slipped away. Once it was off, he quickly covered her with his football shirt to keep her warm. Then he slipped into the kitchen and turned on the taps.

In less than ten minutes, the blanket was washed and Eric spread it over a chair to dry.

'Please let it work!' he muttered, before he went into the living room and sat next to the sleeping baby.

It was six o'clock before he woke up. Mum was standing over him holding the baby.

'What happened, Eric? I went to the baby's room and she wasn't there. I had the fright of my life!'

Eric rubbed his eyes and tried to think of something.

'Er . . . I heard her crying in the night so I brought her down and gave her a bottle. I did it just like you do.'

'Well, you do surprise me!'

'I thought you needed a good night's sleep.'

'Oh, Eric,' she said, blinking away a tear. 'You can be so helpful.'

Then he remembered the blanket.

'Oh yes . . . She was a bit sick. You know how babies are. So I washed that cover thing Auntie Rose sent her.'

Mum was so impressed that Eric changed his mind about running away. Maybe things had started to look up.

TEN

As it turned out, the baby didn't speak to Eric again. The washing must have worked.

'That's a load off your mind, Ez,' said Wesley when they met in the park on Sunday.

'But what about the band, Wez? Am I really out of it?

'No way!' Wez said as he slapped Eric on the shoulder. 'I talked to Kylie and Kelvin yesterday. Told them you were having a bad time cos of the new baby. Kelvin said his mum was really ratty when their baby was born. Kylie said the same. They know what kids have to put up with, Ez.'

It was a great relief!

After that, things began to go smoothly. The baby slept during the night and Eric's band rehearsed at Kelvin's house. All was well.

The final of the Battle of the Bands competition was to be held on Saturday and Wez's mum arrived to pick him up in her car.

'We'll see you later, Eric,' said The Bodge as they waved him off.

'Good luck!' Mum called.

Once they'd reached the theatre, they were shown around and were allowed to go onto the stage to see how it felt. It was large and square and lit by huge bright lights. They walked around trying to take it all in.

'Wow!' said Eric. 'This is cool!'

Kylie grinned and nodded. 'Now I know what it feels like to be famous!'

But Wez and Kelvin were more nervous than they had ever been in their lives.

When the Battle of the Bands started, The Ez Effect was to be the last to play. When it was almost time to go on stage, they stood in the wings waiting for their turn, peeping through the curtain and looking at the audience.

'I can see your mum and The Bodge,' said Kelvin.

'Where?'

'Right at the back.'

Eric peered out. Sure enough, they were there and Mum was holding the baby, wrapped in Auntie Rose's blanket. No problem! thought Eric. Everything was OK now.

At that point, the stage manager called over to them, 'Right, kids. When the last band leaves the stage, I want you to walk on.'

The Evil Five finished their number, the audience cheered and the curtains closed. Then The Ez Effect walked on.

'Good luck, guys!' said Kylie as she sat behind the drum kit. And the curtains opened.

It was the best night of Eric's life so far. He played brilliantly. As did the rest of the band.

Afterwards, they went and sat in the front row waiting for the results.

The judge took his time and made a boring speech while Eric squirmed with impatience. At last, he announced, 'The winning band is . . . The Ez Effect.'

Eric leaped into the air like a cork from a bottle. He jumped and cheered and generally went wild.

Later, when they went backstage for the celebrations, Mum, The Bodge and the baby went, too, and made a great fuss of him.

There was lots of food and cola and Eric thought it was a great party.

'I think a reporter wants to talk to you, Eric,' said Mum as he was stuffing a sandwich into his mouth. 'Just remember, you're a pop star, now!' And she laughed.

Eric brushed the crumbs off his T-shirt, ready to speak to the journalist.

'This is your family, is it, Eric?' the man asked as he opened his notebook.

Eric shrugged his shoulders and said, 'Yeah,' in a cool, pop-starish kind of way.

The reporter jotted some notes and then he noticed the baby. 'And who is this little person?' he asked.

'My sister,' said Eric. 'Actually, she's the band's mascot.' He had just thought of that off the top of his head. Reporters liked that kind of thing.

'Great!' said the journalist and scribbled more notes. 'What's her name?'

Mum leaned forward. 'We only decided today,' she said. 'We think we're going to call her Rose after my sister.'

Eric suddenly felt nervous. One Rose in the family was more than enough.

'Maybe we should talk about it, Mum,' he said.

But the baby shook her head, looked Eric straight in the eye and winked!